Written by
Steven and Susan Traugh

Editor: Kim Cernek
Illustrator: Darcy Tom
Cover Illustrator: Rick Grayson
Designer/Production: Moonhee Pak/Carrie Rickmond
Cover Designer: Barbara Peterson
Art Director: Tom Cochrane
Project Director: Stephanie Oberc

Table of Contents

♫ SONGS AND ACTIVITIES

Introduction

Mother Goose Brain Boost uses the natural benefits of music and movement to enhance your regular preschool and early elementary program. This resource emphasizes the latest research in brain development to help children develop the cognitive skills they need to read and succeed in school.

The 24 nursery rhymes and traditional songs in *Mother Goose Brain Boost* are sung to a variety of delightful rhythms. As children sing, dance, and respond in other ways to the music they hear, critical connections in their brains are formed. The songs and coordinating activities in this resource encourage children to use a number of senses during each learning experience so that information will enter their brains through various pathways. The direct benefit is that children develop essential cognitive skills necessary for success with reading, writing, math, science, and social studies.

This book presents 48 activities that are connected to state standards for early learning. Children will sing, move, listen, and play homemade instruments as they explore concepts such as numbers and counting; directional words; letters and rhyming; sequence and comprehension; time and money; and science and social studies.

All 24 songs are recorded on two separate CDs. The first features lyrics and the second is instumental only. The words for each song are printed on individual reproducible pages, and two activities complement each song. Each activity includes a description of how to enhance brain development as well as complete lists of skills, materials, and step-by-step directions for implementing the activity.

Nursery rhymes and other traditional songs are an important part of every early childhood program. These tunes have stood the test of time because their rhythms and lyrics are easily recalled and fun to repeat. *Mother Goose Brain Boost* shows you new ways to use these old favorites to bolster children's thinking skills.

How Music Enhances Brain Development

The latest research on music in the classroom supports the following ideas:

♪ Music instruction enhances a child's ability to perform skills necessary for reading, including listening; anticipating; and developing memory, recall, and concentration.

♪ Music inspires movement activities that help children "cross the midline." This is the ability to move one hand, foot, or eye into the space of the other hand, foot, or eye. This skill is essential for the left-right orientation required for reading and writing.

♪ Music develops the areas of the brain that are responsible for emotion and memory.

♪ Music and movement activities help children demonstrate self-control. Young children become thoughtful about how and when they move their bodies and use their voices when they participate in music-related activities.

♪ Music and movement activities introduce children to language and sensory-motor skills simultaneously.

♪ Children develop logic and rhythmic skills when they keep the beat of a song. These skills increase a child's ability to solve problems.

♪ Music facilitates first- and second-language acquisition because it allows language to enter the brain through several different pathways.

♪ Children with musical experiences generally understand fractions and proportional math better.

♪ Music helps children develop spatial-temporal ability, which is the ability to transform objects in space and time. This helps a child understand fractions, geometry, and proportional math.

♪ Music facilitates participation in related activities that enhance the development of social, language, and motor skills.

What You Can Do in Your Classroom

To enhance the benefits music has on learning, keep some of the following ideas in mind when organizing your classroom:

♪ Develop a print-rich room. Display enlarged copies of the reproducible song sheets to help children track the words of the song as the recording plays.

♪ Play with words and sounds. The rhymes in these songs give children the phonemic awareness practice they need. Bind copies of the reproducible lyrics into class songbooks, and place them in your classroom library so that children can "sing," and eventually read, their favorite rhymes.

♪ Rewrite, rewrite, rewrite. These nursery rhymes have stood the test of time because they excite young listeners so completely. Rewrite a rhyme to reflect your current unit of study, and then sing your song to the corresponding instrumental track.

♪ Exercise the body and mind. Each song is accompanied by a theme-based physical exercise to boost brainpower. These research-based exercises take less than a minute to do yet they can make a lifetime of difference to a young learner. Use the suggested activities as a morning warm-up or during transitional time, and watch remarkable things happen.

Meeting Standards

SONG TITLES	One Elephant Went out to Play	Five Little Monkeys	This Old Man	One, Two, Buckle My Shoe	Teddy Bear, Teddy Bear	Eency-Weency Spider	Humpty Dumpty	Down by the Station	A-Hunting We Will Go	Wee Willie Winkie	Down by the Bay	There Was a Crooked Man	Peanut Butter and Jelly	Mary Had a Little Lamb	The Little Turtle	Little Miss Muffet	Hickory Dickory Dock	Six Little Ducks	Pop! Goes the Weasel	Sing a Song of Sixpence	Little Boy Blue	Old MacDonald Had a Farm	Hey Diddle Diddle	The Cat Came Piping out of the Barn
READING READINESS																								
Listen	•	•		•				•	•	•	•		•		•			•	•			•		
Sequence			•					•					•	•	•		•							
Indentify letters													•											•
Identify beginning sounds			•										•						•					
Identify rhyming words			•	•					•		•		•											
Isolate beginning sounds										•			•						•				•	
Substitute beginning sounds			•						•	•														
Understand left-to-right orientation								•				•	•	•	•									
Understand one-to-one correspondence								•				•												
Understand opposite word pairs	•																•							
Understand directional words								•																
Learn new vocabulary words	•	•		•		•			•	•			•					•	•				•	
MATH																								
Recognize numbers from 1-10																	•		•			•		
Count		•															•			•	•			
Sort																		•					•	
Make patterns			•																			•		
Understand size relationships														•		•						•		
Analyze data																				•				
Add		•																						

SONG TITLES	One Elephant Went out to Play	Five Little Monkeys	This Old Man	One, Two, Buckle My Shoe	Teddy Bear, Teddy Bear	Eency-Weency Spider	Humpty Dumpty	Down by the Station	A-Hunting We Will Go	Wee Willie Winkie	Down by the Bay	There Was a Crooked Man	Peanut Butter and Jelly	Mary Had a Little Lamb	The Little Turtle	Little Miss Muffet	Hickory Dickory Dock	Six Little Ducks	Pop! Goes the Weasel	Sing a Song of Sixpence	Little Boy Blue	Old MacDonald Had a Farm	Hey Diddle Diddle	The Cat Came Piping out of the Barn
SOCIAL STUDIES																								
Learn about community workers									•															
Make comparisons																			•	•	•	•	•	
FINE MOTOR SKILLS																								
Hold a crayon and pencil correctly				•						•		•	•		•						•			•
Hold and use scissors correctly				•																	•			
Trace																	•							
Print name				•		•						•	•				•							
GROSS MOTOR SKILLS																								
Run		•																						
Improve balance	•				•																			
Jump		•																	•					
Track objects	•													•										
Throw and catch a ball																								•
Improve coordination	•	•						•									•							
MUSIC AND MOVEMENT SKILLS																								
Sing		•	•		•	•												•						
Understand rhythm			•					•	•		•			•									•	
Concentrate	•	•			•				•							•								
Follow directions	•	•	•	•	•	•	•	•		•		•	•		•		•			•	•	•		•
March								•																
Keep a steady beat								•	•					•										•

Song Styles

ONE ELEPHANT WENT OUT TO PLAY

This song is set in an African style that features flutes, drums, and percussion instruments. Voices and instruments are added to the arrangement as each additional elephant comes out to play and subtracted as each elephant is called away.

FIVE LITTLE MONKEYS

This rock shuffle arrangement opens with horns, organ, piano, guitars, bass, drums, and percussion. The arrangement gradually thins as each monkey falls off the bed in turn.

THIS OLD MAN

This counting song/movement game is set in a reggae style that features pan flute, marimba, steel drums, bass, and drums.

ONE, TWO, BUCKLE MY SHOE

This counting chant with variations features claps, snaps, drums, and percussion instruments in a Brazilian samba style.

TEDDY BEAR, TEDDY BEAR

This poem has been turned into a lullaby that features the harp with string orchestra. The melody is introduced as an echo song and then sung in unison.

EENCY-WEENCY SPIDER

This song features the percussion section in an orchestral march. Children are encouraged to do the movements as they sing. The style then switches to swing, featuring piano, bass, and drums for the conclusion of the activity.

DOWN BY THE STATION

Beginning with a train whistle, this song accelerates into playful reggae style. The song is first presented as an echo, then done in unison, and finally performed as a round.

HUMPTY DUMPTY

This piece uses the same orchestration and Baroque style as Handel's *Music for a Royal Fireworks*. The musical style is intended to match the poem's teasing reference to "all the king's horses and all the king's men."

A-HUNTING WE WILL GO

This song opens with the traditional hunting-horn call, followed by a galloping classical orchestral arrangement that builds and transforms into a jazz treatment of the song.

THERE WAS A CROOKED MAN

Set in a Louisiana Cajun style, this song features *concertina* (small accordion), guitar, bass, drums, and percussion. The melody is first presented as an echo song, then performed in unison.

WEE WILLIE WINKIE

The arrangement for this poem was inspired by Hayden's *Clock Symphony*. The poem is first performed as a chant in time with the music, then turned into a song with chamber orchestra accompaniment.

DOWN BY THE BAY

Set in a New Orleans jazz style, this song presents playful lyric variations at tempos that alternate between relaxed and ragtime.

MARY HAD A LITTLE LAMB

Set to a driving country beat, this song features harmonica, banjo, piano, bass, drums, and a barnyard full of animals.

THE LITTLE TURTLE

This chant is set to a rock shuffle beat that features a variety of drums and percussion instruments. The verse is first presented as an echo chant, then a movement game, and finally as a unison chant with movements.

LITTLE MISS MUFFET

This nursery rhyme is accompanied by a solo harpsichord with music written in the Baroque style of J.S. Bach. The rhyme is first set as a chant, followed by a movement game, and finally performed as a song.

PEANUT BUTTER AND JELLY

Set in a Cuban salsa style, this poem is first presented as an echo chant that features conga drums, bass, and percussion. The addition of horns expands the rhyme.

HICKORY DICKORY DOCK

Done in a light ballet style, this song presents a collection of sounds, including gears, springs, wheels, and chimes.

SIX LITTLE DUCKS

Done as a classical march in the style of *Peter and the Wolf*, this song features flute, oboe, clarinet, bassoon, fanfare trumpets, and percussion.

POP! GOES THE WEASEL

This song is set in an East African style that features flute, xylophone, timpani, drums, and percussion.

SING A SONG OF SIXPENCE

Done in a Renaissance troubadour style, this song opens with a solo guitar and then adds drums, tambourine, and oboe.

THE CAT CAME PIPING OUT OF THE BARN

Set as an Irish bagpipe dance, this piece features bagpipes, *boudron* (Irish drum), flute, guitar, fiddle, bass, and drums.

OLD MACDONALD HAD A FARM

This additive song alternates male and female voices set in contrasting rock-n-roll styles from the '50s and '70s.

LITTLE BOY BLUE

Naturally, this music features a wide array of horns, including trumpets, trombones, French horns, and tuba.

HEY DIDDLE DIDDLE

The country fiddle arrangement presents the rhyme first as a chant, then introduces movements, and finally turns the rhyme into a song.

One Elephant Went out to Play

One elephant went out to play
Out on a spider's web one day.
He had such enormous fun.
He called for another elephant to come.

Two elephants went out to play
Out on a spider's web one day.
They had such enormous fun.
They called for another elephant to come.

Three elephants went out to play
Out on a spider's web one day.
They had such enormous fun.
They called for another elephant to come.

Four elephants went out to play
Out on a spider's web one day.
They had such enormous fun.
They called for another elephant to come.

Five elephants went out to play
Out on a spider's web one day.
They had such enormous fun.
Playing all together in the sun.

Five elephants had so much fun
Until a mother called for one.
He had to go and clean the floor.
Take 1 away from 5 and you get 4.

Four elephants had so much fun
Until a mother called for one.
She had to go and have some tea.
Take 1 away from 4 and you get 3.

Three elephants had so much fun
Until a mother called for one.
He had to go and find his shoe.
Take 1 away from 3 and you get 2.

Two elephants had so much fun
Until a mother called for one.
She had to go and get chores done.
Take 1 away from 2 and you get 1.

One elephant had so much fun
Until his mother called her son.
He had to go and eat a ton.
Take 1 away from 1 and you get none.

Mother Goose Brain Boost © 2006 Creative Teaching Press

Trunk Tracking

Tell children to hold their arms straight out in front of them. Show children how to clasp their hands together and press their pointer fingers together to form an elephant trunk. Ask them to use their "trunk" to form a long, thin figure eight. Encourage children to focus on the end of their fingers and use their eyes to follow the entire path of the "eight." Play "One Elephant Went out to Play" as children practice this skill.

SKILLS

Follow directions
Listen
Track objects

MATERIALS

• "One Elephant Went out to Play"
  (CD 1, Track 1)

Web Walking

Use jump ropes or yarn to create a "web." Invite children to walk along the ropes of the web. Give them simple commands to introduce new vocabulary words, directional words, and opposite word pairs. For example, tell children to move in and out, on and off, forward and backward, and quickly or slowly as they explore the web.

SKILLS

Concentrate
Improve balance
Improve coordination
Learn new vocabulary words
Understand opposite word pairs

MATERIALS

• jump ropes or yarn

Five Little Monkeys

Five little monkeys jumping on the bed—
One fell off and bumped his head.
Mother called the doctor, and the doctor said,
"No more monkeys jumping on the bed."

Four little monkeys . . .
Three little monkeys . . .
Two little monkeys . . .
One little monkey . . .

No little monkeys jumping on the bed—
None fell off and bumped his head.
Mother called the doctor, and the doctor said,
"Put those monkeys straight to bed!"

Put Those Monkeys Right to Bed

Give each child a Monkeys Jumping on the Bed reproducible to color and cut apart. Play "Five Little Monkeys," and invite children to use the monkeys to act out the song as they sing along. Tell children to use their cards as you direct them. For example, say *Put one monkey over the bed, put a second monkey on the bed, and put two more monkeys under the bed.* Give all three directions at the same time to help children expand their concentration. Use different number and directional words to repeat the activity.

MATERIALS

- "Five Little Monkeys" (CD 1, Track 2)
- Monkeys Jumping on the Bed reproducible (page 14)
- crayons or markers
- scissors

Monkeys in Motion

Invite children to name other ways a monkey might move, such as roll, hop, or wiggle. Change the words of the song to describe another way the monkeys could move on the bed (e.g., *Five little monkeys rolling on the bed*). Play the instrumental version of the song, and invite children to sing their new verses and act them out.

MATERIALS

- "Five Little Monkeys" (CD 2, Track 2)

Monkeys Jumping on the Bed

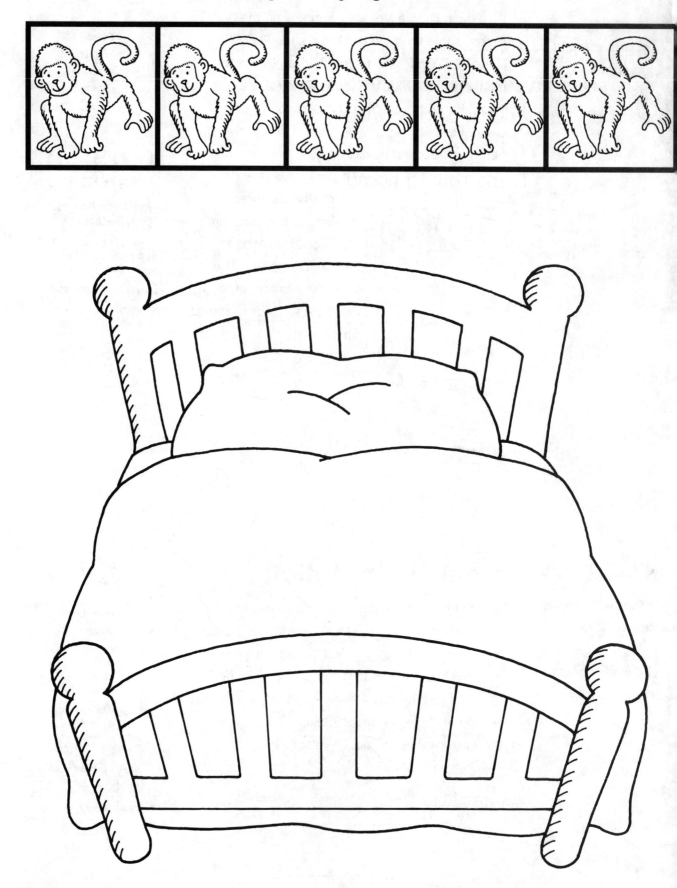

This Old Man

This old man, he played **one**.
He played knick-knack on my **thumb**
With a knick-knack, paddywhack,
Give the dog a bone.
This old man came rolling home.

two/shoe
three/knee
four/door
five/hive
six/sticks
seven/heaven
eight/gate
nine/spine
ten/again

Knick-Knack,
Knick-Knack ...

Name and model various movements as you sing the song to encourage auditory and kinesthetic brain connections.

Paddy-Whack Parade

Play "This Old Man," and invite children to create movements to dramatize each part of the song. Encourage children to name the movements they create. Play the instrumental version of the song, and invite children to sing and perform their movements. Call out the name of each movement to help children recall the pattern and sequence of the movements. Invite children to dance around the room as a group to make a "paddy-whack parade."

Follow directions
Make patterns
Sequence
Sing

MATERIALS

- "This Old Man" (CD 1, Track 3; CD 2, Track 3)

This activity helps children practice phonemic awareness and phonics in a fun, motivating way.

Knick-Knack Nonsense

Copy and cut apart a set of Knick-Knack Nonsense Cards, and place them at a center. Invite children to use the sounds to replace the beginning sounds of the phrase *Knick-knack, paddywhack* to make new nonsense words.

Identify beginning sounds
Identify rhyming words
Substitute beginning sounds

MATERIALS

- Knick-Knack Nonsense Cards (page 17)
- scissors

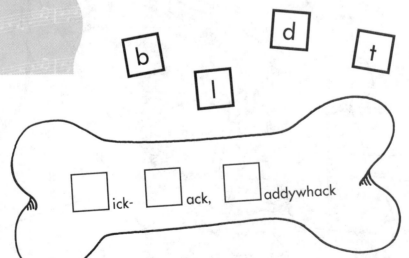

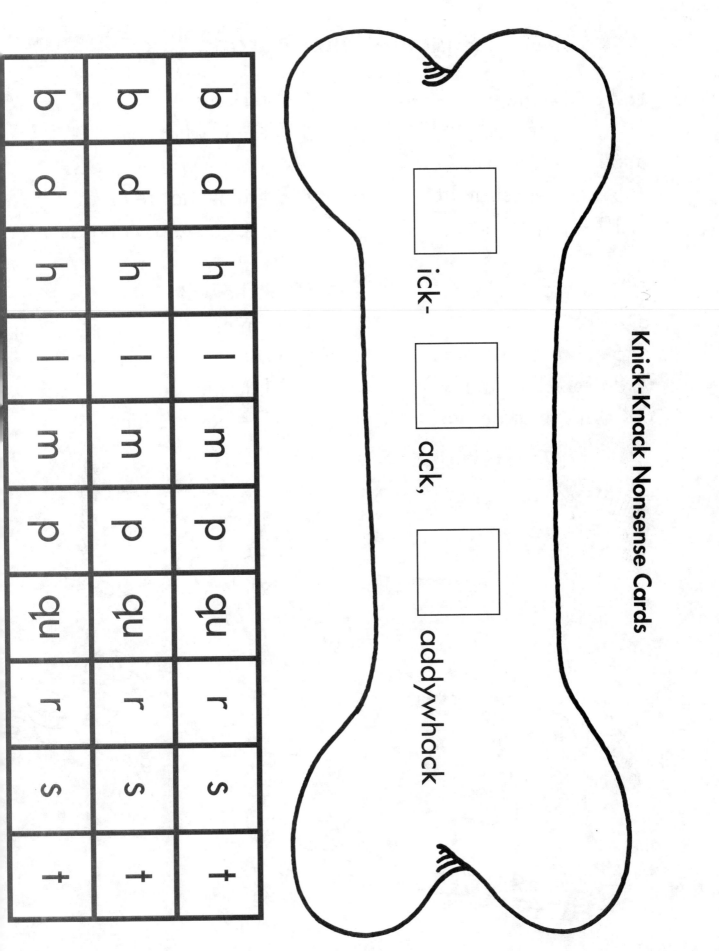

Knick-Knack Nonsense Cards

ick- ack, addywhack

b	d	h	l	m	p	qu	r	s	t
b	d	h	l	m	p	qu	r	s	t
b	d	h	l	m	p	qu	r	s	t

One, Two, Buckle My Shoe

1, 2 Buckle my shoe.
3, 4 Shut the door.
5, 6 Pick up sticks.
7, 8 Lay them straight.
9, 10 A big fat hen.

1, 2 Get some glue.
3, 4 Fix the door.
5, 6 A horse that kicks.
7, 8 Broke the gate.
9, 10 It's fixed again.

1, 2 I like you.
3, 4 Know what for?
5, 6 'Cause you do tricks.
7, 8 I think they're great
9, 10 Can we be friends?

10, 9 The water's fine.
8, 7 I'm in heaven.
6, 5 Let's take a dive.
4, 3 Into the sea.
2, 1 The ocean's fun.

Rhythm Repeat

Give each child a pair of rhythm sticks. Play "One, Two, Buckle My Shoe," and invite children to tap out the beat as they sing along. Show children how to switch the position of their hands so that the hand that was on the bottom is now on the top. Ask children to change their hand position after each verse.

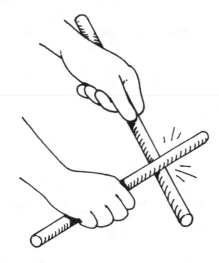

MATERIALS

- "One, Two, Buckle My Shoe" (CD 1, Tracks 4 and 5)
- rhythm sticks

Lyric Link

Write *2, 4, 6, 8,* and *10* on separate index cards, and scatter them on the floor. Make an enlarged copy of the Rhyming Words reproducible, cut apart the cards, and place them in a box. Invite a child to draw a card from the box. Ask the child to name the picture of the card (e.g., *oar*) and decide which number rhymes with it (e.g., *four*). Encourage the child to place the word card beside the matching number card. Have the class sing the line from "One, Two, Buckle My Shoe" that features that number (e.g., *Three, four, shut the door*). Invite a different child to draw a card and repeat the activity until no cards remain.

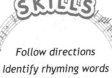

MATERIALS

- Rhyming Words reproducible (page 20)
- index cards
- scissors
- box

Rhyming Words

shoe

glue

door

oar

bricks

chicks

plate

skate

pen

hen

Teddy Bear, Teddy Bear

Teddy bear, teddy bear, turn around.
Teddy bear, teddy bear, touch the ground.

Teddy bear, teddy bear, show your shoe.
Teddy bear, teddy bear, that will do.

Teddy bear, teddy bear, go to bed.
Teddy bear, teddy bear, rest your head.

Teddy bear, teddy bear, turn out the light.
Teddy bear, teddy bear, say good night.

Good night...

Teddy Bear Balance

Invite children to stand at arm's length from each other. Play "Teddy Bear, Teddy Bear." Ask children to raise their left leg and their right arm and balance as you count to ten. Invite children to repeat the activity with the right leg and left arm. Try other variations of this activity, such as hand to knee (in front), hand to knee (behind), elbow to knee, or hand to foot.

Follow directions
Improve balance
Concentrate

MATERIALS

- "Teddy Bear, Teddy Bear" (CD 1, Track 6)

Teddy Bear Band

Cut a hole in the top of a shoebox, and tape the lid to the box. Stretch several rubber bands of different widths across the opening. Invite children to pluck the rubber bands, and encourage them to describe the different tones they hear. Play "Teddy Bear, Teddy Bear," and invite children to play and sing along.

Listen
Sing

MATERIALS

- "Teddy Bear, Teddy Bear" (CD 1, Track 6)
- scissors
- shoebox
- tape
- rubber bands

Eency-Weency Spider

The eency-weency spider
Went up the water spout.

Down came the rain
And washed the spider out.

Out came the sun
And dried up all the rain.

And the eency-weency spider
Went up the spout again.

Children learn to focus, listen, and become self-reliant when they follow the directions in this activity.

Sequencing the Spider's Every Step

Follow directions
Hold and use scissors correctly
Print name

Give each child a paper plate to paint black. Allow the paint to dry. Give each child a Spider Sequence reproducible to color. Tell children to write their name on the blank line in the rectangle, cut out the rectangle, and glue it to the top of their black plate. Ask children to cut out the circle from their paper. Give each child another paper plate, have children glue their circle to it. Help children place their black plate on their white plate, and connect them in the center with a brass fastener. Cut a triangle out of each child's black plate so that one "wedge" on the white plate is revealed. Have children accordion-fold eight black construction paper strips and glue them to the bottom plate to make legs. Play "Eency-Weency Spider." Invite children to turn the top part of their spider to reveal the picture as it is named in the song.

MATERIALS

- "Eency-Weency Spider" (CD 1, Track 7)
- Spider Sequence reproducible (page 25)
- paper plates
- black tempera paint
- paintbrushes
- crayons
- scissors
- glue
- brass fasteners
- black construction paper strips

Children will use oral, kinesthetic, and visual modalities to learn new vocabulary.

A Spider's Song and Dance

Follow directions
Hold a crayon correctly
Hold and use scissors correctly
Sing

Give each child a House reproducible to color and a Sun and Rain reproducible to color and cut apart. Use scissors to make a slit above and below the slit on each child's house. Give each child a plastic spider and a piece of yarn. Help children tie their spider to the center of their yarn. Show them how to insert the top and the bottom of the yarn through the slits in their house and tie both ends of the yarn together. Have children place the sun and rain cutout behind their house. Help them insert a brass fastener through the slit in the center of both papers to connect them. Play "Eency-Weency Spider," and invite children to manipulate their paper as they sing the song.

MATERIALS

- "Eency-Weency Spider" (CD 1, Track 7)
- House reproducible (page 26)
- Sun and Rain reproducible (page 27)
- crayons or markers
- scissors
- plastic spiders, yarn, brass fasteners

Spider Sequence

The Eency-Weency Spider

by _____

House

Sun and Rain

Humpty Dumpty

Humpty Dumpty sat on a wall.
Humpty Dumpty had a great fall.
All the king's horses
And all the king's men
Couldn't put Humpty together again.

Humpty Dumpty started to roll.
Humpty Dumpty fell in a hole.
All the king's men
Went searching about
'Til a brown little mole pushed and
rolled him back out.

Humpty Dumpty fell in a nest.
Humpty Dumpty had a great rest.
The king found it absurd
That an old mother bird
Knew how to heal Humpty Dumpty
the best.

Egg Rolls

Arrange for children to sit on a padded surface. Ask children to lie on their back and pull their knees into their chest and clasp their fingers across their legs to form an "egg." Tell children to gently rock forward and back along the entire length of their spine. Have children repeat the exercise using a side-to-side movement. Play "Humpty Dumpty," and have children repeat the exercises.

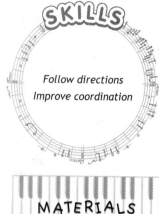

SKILLS

Follow directions
Improve coordination

MATERIALS

- "Humpty Dumpty" (CD 1, Track 8)

Humpty Dumpty Dance

Write past tense verbs (e.g., *danced*, *hopped*, *slept*) on separate strips of paper, and place each one in a separate plastic egg. Prepare one egg for every two children. Divide the class into pairs, and have partners sit a few feet apart on the floor facing each other. Give one child in each pair an egg. Play "Humpty Dumpty," and invite the partners to roll their egg back and forth as they sing the song. At the end of the song, invite one pair of children to open their egg and remove the slip of paper. Read aloud the word on the paper, and invite children to substitute the new word for the word *sat* in the first verse of "Humpty Dumpty." For example, children could sing *Humpty Dumpty danced on a wall*. Play the instrumental version of "Humpty Dumpty," and invite children to sing the new verse as they roll their egg back and forth. Repeat the activity until each pair of children has opened their egg.

SKILLS

Follow directions
Learn new vocabulary words

MATERIALS

- "Humpty Dumpty" (CD 1, Track 8; CD 2, Track 7)
- paper strips
- plastic eggs

Down by the Station

Down by the station, early in the morning,
See the little puffer bellies all in a row.
See the engine driver pull the little throttle.
Chug! Chug! Puff! Puff! Off they go.

Children will follow directions and learn directional words as they move to a beat.

Puffer Belly Beat

Follow directions
Keep a steady beat
March
Understand directional words
Understand rhythm

Arrange children in a line, and ask them to place one hand on the waist of the child in front of them. Tell children to use their other hand to simulate a train wheel. Play "Down by the Station," and encourage children to make "chug" and "puff" sounds as they move around the room. Use directional words to complete the frame *Puffer belly, puffer belly, move to the _____*. Direct children to go left, right, forward, straight, in a circle, or backward. Use a drum or tambourine to indicate when children should begin moving, and continue beating the instrument with a slow beat as they move. Slowly increase and decrease the tempo of the beat, and encourage children to move according to the varying rate.

MATERIALS

- "Down by the Station" (CD 1, Track 9)
- drum or tambourine

Children will identify that individual words make sentences and that we read sentences from left to right.

All Aboard with Sight Words

Follow directions
Print name
Sequence
Understand left-to-right orientation
Understand one-to-one correspondence

Give each child a Train Cars reproducible and a piece of construction paper. Invite children to write their name on the engine. Ask each child to dictate a five-word sentence to you, and write one word on each train car. For example, children could say *Carmen rides the red train* or *The big train goes fast*. Tell children to cut out their train cars. Help children glue their cars in the correct order on the construction paper.

MATERIALS

- Train Cars reproducible (page 32)
- construction paper
- scissors
- glue

Train Cars

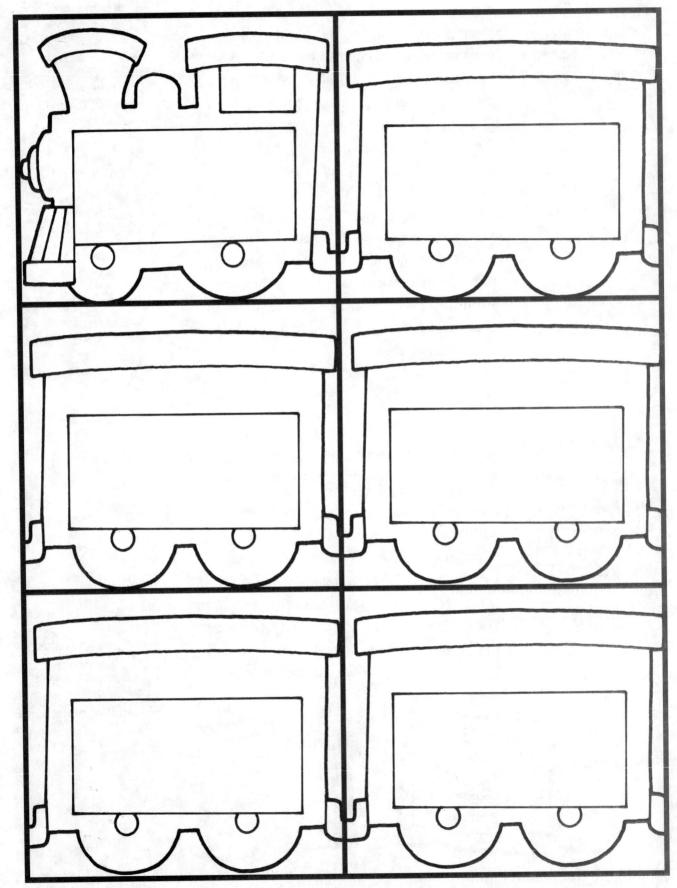

Mother Goose Brain Boost © 2006 Creative Teaching Press

A-Hunting We Will Go

Oh, a-hunting we will go.
A-hunting we will go.
We'll catch a fox
And put him in a box,
And then we'll let him go!

Other Verses
We'll catch a cat
And put him in a hat.

We'll catch a mouse
And put him in a house.

We'll catch a goat
And put him in a boat.

We'll catch a bear
And take him to the fair.

We'll catch a mongoose
And feed him apple juice.

We'll catch a stegosaurus
And make him dance for us.

We'll catch a hippopotamus
And try and put him on the bus.

Children will manipulate sounds to make new words.

Hunting for Words

Identify rhyming words
Substitute beginning sounds

Play "A-Hunting We Will Go," and ask children to name the pairs of rhyming words they hear in the song. Give each child a Sight Word Flip Books reproducible to color. Show children how to cut out the letters *b* and *c* below the word *hat*. Help children place both letters on top of the *h*, and staple them at the top to make a flip book. Repeat with the other half of the paper to make a flip book with the word *boat*. Encourage children to read the words in their books to each other.

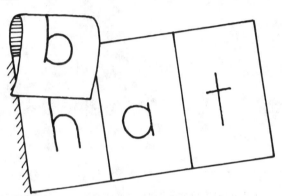

MATERIALS

- "A-Hunting We Will Go" (CD 1, Track 10)
- Sight Word Flip Books reproducible (page 35)
- crayons or markers
- scissors
- stapler

Drumming strengthens a child's audio memory, improves left-brain, right-brain connectivity, and improves pattern recognition.

A-Galloping We Will Go

Concentrate
Keep a steady beat
Listen
Understand rhythm

Give each child two pencils. Show children how to hold the pointed ends and use the eraser ends to make a galloping sound on a table or other hard surface. Have children tap one pencil against the other while you call out the "tah-dum" sound of the gallop. Play "A-Hunting We Will Go," and invite children to tap along. Encourage them to keep switching which hand is on top to help the left and right part of the brain "communicate."

MATERIALS

- "A-Hunting We Will Go" (CD 1, Track 10)
- pencils

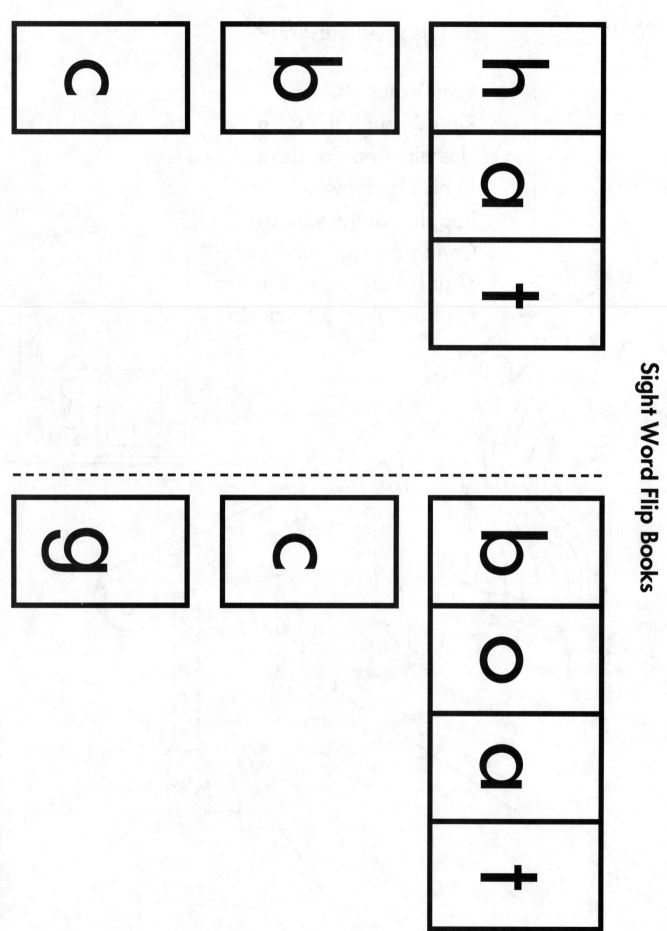

Sight Word Flip Books

Wee Willie Winkie

Wee Willie Winkie
Runs through the town,
Upstairs and downstairs
In his nightgown,
Rapping at the window,
Crying through the lock,
"Are the children all in bed,
For now it's eight o'clock?"

Children will develop fine motor skills as they practice phonemic awareness.

Wee Words

Play "Wee Willie Winkie," and invite children to raise or clap their hands when they hear *Wee Willie Winkie*. Name a letter, and write it on the board. Ask children to make the sound of the letter, and use it in place of the *W* to make new names (e.g., *Bee Billie Binkie* or *Dee Dillie Dinkie*). Give each child a Wee Willie Winkie reproducible. Have children write other letters on it to make more names.

Isolate beginning sounds
Substitute beginning sounds
Listen

MATERIALS

- "Wee Willie Winkie" (CD 1, Track 11)
- Wee Willie Winkie reproducible (page 38)

Children will improve fine motor skills as they explore the people who help them in their community.

Wonderful Wee Workers

Play "Wee Willie Winkie," and ask children if there really is a "wee little person" who checks on children as they sleep. Ask children to name people who really do help keep others safe, and write their ideas on chart paper. Encourage children to describe what each person does. Have children draw pictures of these community workers, and write the title of each person below children's drawings. Tell children to write their name on their paper. Place each child's drawing in a pile. Make a copy of the Wee Willie Winkie song page, and use it as the first page of the class book. Bind the papers together under a construction paper cover titled *Wonderful Wee Workers*.

Hold a crayon and pencil correctly
Learn about community workers
Listen

MATERIALS

- "Wee Willie Winkie" (CD 1, Track 11)
- chart paper
- drawing paper
- crayons or markers
- bookbinding materials (e.g., stapler or hole punch and yarn or curling ribbon)
- construction paper

Wee Willie Winkie

b	d	f	h	j	k	l	m
n	p	r	s	t	v	y	z

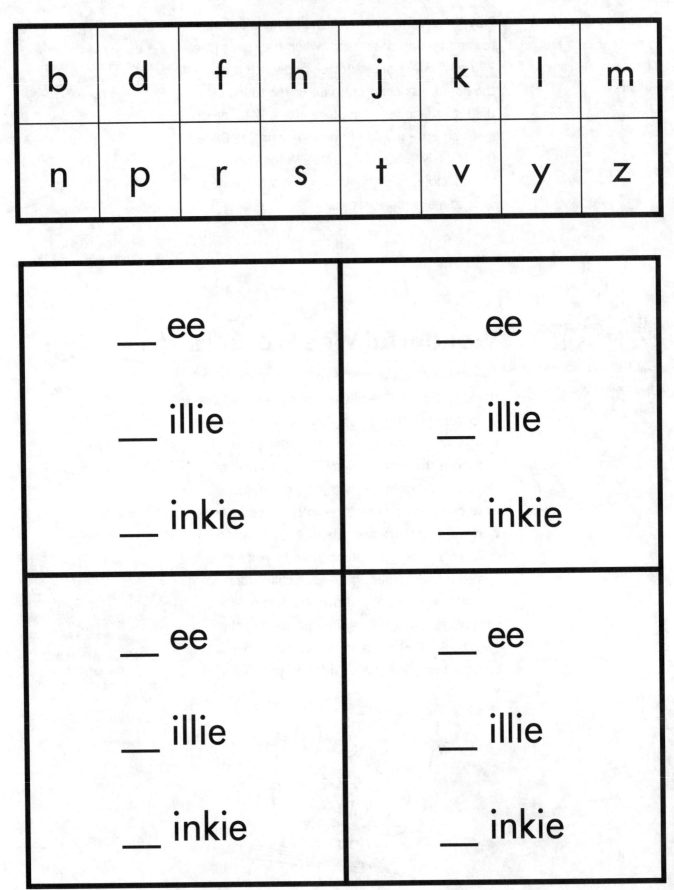

__ ee

__ illie

__ inkie

__ ee

__ illie

__ inkie

__ ee

__ illie

__ inkie

__ ee

__ illie

__ inkie

Mother Goose Brain Boost © 2006 Creative Teaching Press

Down by the Bay

Down by the bay
Where the watermelons grow,
Back to my home
I dare not go,
For if I do
My mother will say,
"Did you ever seen a whale with a polka-dot tail?
Down by the bay."

Other Verses
Did you ever see a goose kissing a moose?
Did you ever see a bear combing his hair?
Did you ever see a hog learning to jog?
Did you ever see a snake eat a birthday cake?
Did you ever see a fly making apple pie?

Down by My Bay

Give each child a slice of watermelon to eat. Ask children to save their seeds. Wash and dry the seeds. Cut paper plates in half, and give each child two paper plate halves. Show children how to place their watermelon seeds between their paper plates, and staple them together to make a "tambourine." Have children paint their tambourine green along the edge to make a watermelon rind and red in the middle to make the pulp. Have them add black dots to make seeds. Allow the paint to dry. Play "Down by the Bay," and encourage children to hold their tambourine with one hand and beat it with the other hand as they sing. Ask them to alternate which hand holds the tambourine and which one beats on it to promote left/right brain development. Ask children to think of additional silly pairs of rhyming words they could add to the song. Play the instrumental version of the song, and invite children to play their tambourine as they sing their new verses.

MATERIALS

- "Down by the Bay" (CD 1, Track 12; CD 2 Track 11)
- watermelon slices
- scissors
- paper plates
- stapler
- green, red, and black paint
- paintbrushes

Down by the Bay Mini-Books

Give each child a Down by the Bay reproducible to cut apart. Ask children to arrange the pieces in order, and staple them together to make a book. Play "Down by the Bay," and ask children to name silly pairs of rhyming words from the song. Invite children to name their own pair of silly words, and write them on the blank lines of their book. Encourage children to read their books to each other.

MATERIALS

- "Down by the Bay" (CD 1, Track 12)
- Down by the Bay reproducible (page 41)
- scissors
- stapler
- crayons

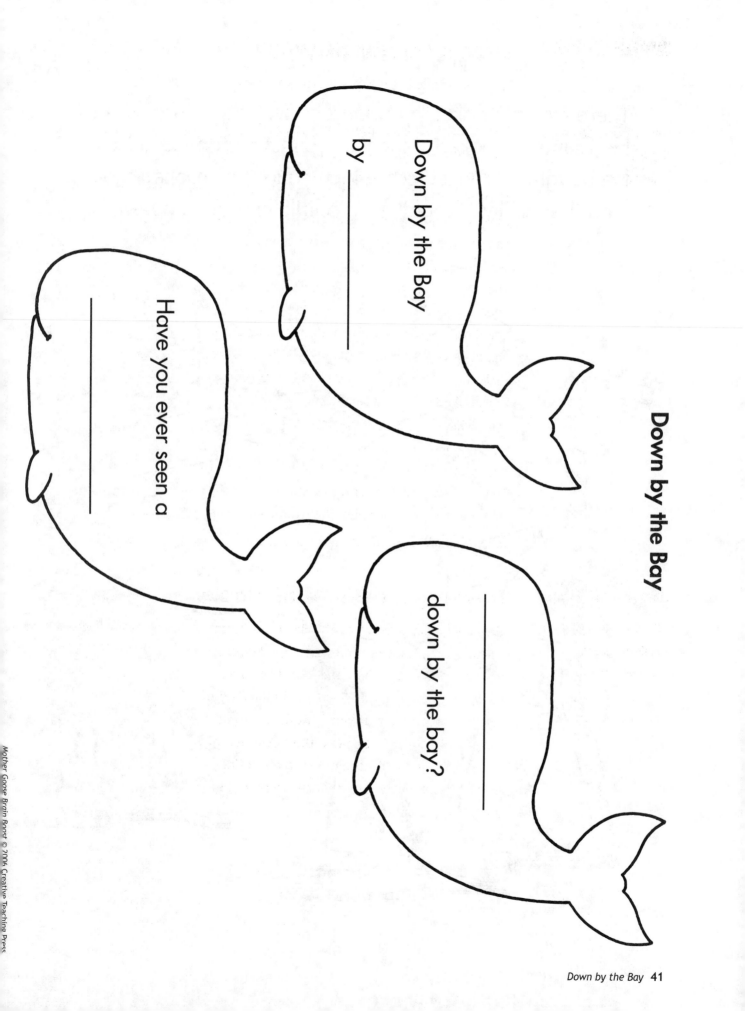

Down by the Bay

Down by the Bay

by _____

Have you ever seen a _____

down by the bay? _____

There Was a Crooked Man

There was a crooked man, and he walked a crooked mile.
He found a crooked sixpence against a crooked stile.
He bought a crooked cat, which caught a crooked mouse.
And they all lived together in a little crooked house.

This activity promotes kinesthetic learning of letters.

Crooked Letter Lines

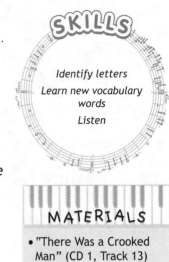
Play "There Was a Crooked Man," and discuss with children the vocabulary in the song. Explain that *crooked* means "bent." Give each child a jump rope, and ask children to make a line with it. Encourage children to adjust their line to make it "crooked." Explain that the letters of the alphabet are crooked lines too. Show children how to use their rope to form an S. Challenge children to form other letters, and encourage them to name each other's letters.

MATERIALS

- "There Was a Crooked Man" (CD 1, Track 13)
- jump ropes

Children will develop fine motor skills and practice letter identification as they connect the dots.

Crooked House

Give each child a Crooked House reproducible. Tell children to write their name at the top of their paper. Invite children to use a pencil to connect the dots to see where the crooked man and his cat live.

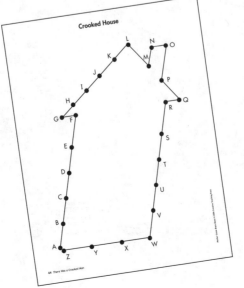

MATERIALS

- Crooked House reproducible (page 44)

Crooked House

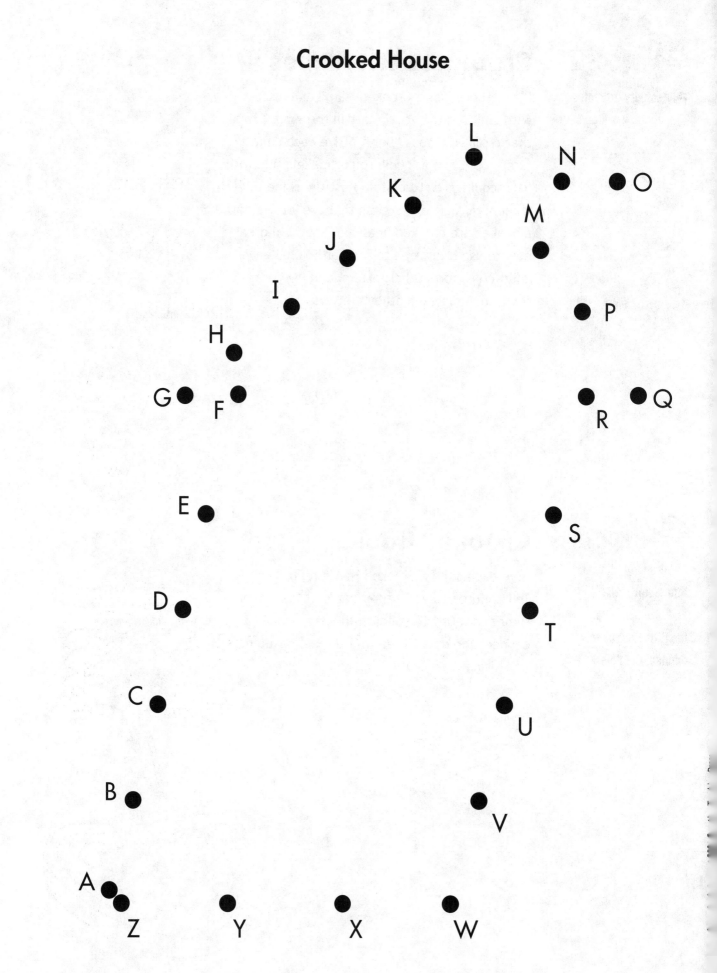

Peanut Butter and Jelly

Chant

Peanut, peanut butter, jelly, jelly.

First you take the peanuts, and you crush 'em, crush 'em.

Peanut, peanut butter, jelly, jelly.

Then you take the grapes, and you squish 'em, squish 'em.

Peanut, peanut butter, jelly, jelly.

Then you take the bread and you spread it, spread it.

Peanut, peanut butter, jelly, jelly.

Then you make a sandwich, and you eat it, eat it.

Peanut, peanut butter, jelly, jelly.

Then You Make a Sandwich

Play "Peanut Butter and Jelly," and encourage children to sing along. Give each child a First and Then reproducible to color. Show children how to cut apart the picture cards. Ask children *What is the beginning sound of the word **First**?* Tell them to point to the word that begins with *F* on their paper. Encourage children to guess what the word above the second column says. Invite children to describe the pictures in the first column. Point to the picture of the peanuts, and say *First you take the peanuts. Then you* . . . . Ask children to find the picture card that illustrates what to do with the peanuts, and have them glue it beside the first picture. Encourage children to use the line from the song to describe the picture (e.g., *First you take the peanuts. Then you crush 'em.*). Repeat with the remaining cards, and then review the sequence of events in the song.

SKILLS

Identify beginning sounds

Identify rhyming words

Isolate beginning sounds

Sequence

MATERIALS

- "Peanut Butter and Jelly" (CD 1, Track 14)
- First and Then reproducible (page 47)
- crayons
- scissors
- glue

Perfect Pairs

Explain to children that peanut butter and jelly are often paired together. Ask children to name other pairs of objects they know, such as salt and pepper and the sun and the moon. Give each child a Pairs reproducible. Tell children to write their name at the top of their paper. Ask them to use their pencil to point to the picture of the sun at the top of the page and then draw a line across to connect the sun and the moon. Then, tell children to place their pencil on the table. Show them how to tap their left hand on the table and say *sun* and then tap their right hand on the table and say *moon*. Repeat with the remaining pictures.

SKILLS

Understand left-to-right orientation

Print name

Hold a pencil correctly

Learn new vocabulary words

MATERIALS

- Pairs reproducible (page 48)

First and Then

First   Then

Pairs

Mary Had a Little Lamb

Mary had a little lamb,
Little lamb, little lamb.
Mary had a little lamb.
Its fleece was white as snow.

And everywhere that Mary went,
Mary went, Mary went.
Everywhere that Mary went
The lamb was sure to go.

It followed her to school one day,
School one day, school one day.
It followed her to school one day.
That was against the rule.

It made the children laugh and play,
Laugh and play, laugh and play.
It made the children laugh and play
To see a lamb at school.

The teacher said, "What shall we do?
Shall we do? Shall we do?"
The teacher said, "What shall we do?
This lamb has come to school."

Let's teach her how to read and write,
Read and write, read and write.
Let's teach her how to read and write
And learn the golden rule.

Mary's lamb now teaches school,
Teaches school, teaches school.
Mary's lamb now teaches school
On her grandpa's farm.

Children will develop left-to-right orientation, an essential skill for tracking print, as they put objects in order by ascending size.

A Lamb at School

Understand left-to-right orientation
Sequence
Understand size relationships

Play "Mary Had a Little Lamb." Ask children to name animals that might live on a farm. Give each child a Farm Animals reproducible to color and cut apart. Give each child a large sheet of green construction paper. Tell children to arrange their farm animals from smallest to largest from left-to-right on the "meadow." Check children's work, and then have them glue their animals in place on their paper. Encourage children to add a barn, a fence, and flowers to their background.

MATERIALS

- "Mary Had a Little Lamb" (CD 1, Track 15)
- Farm Animals reproducible (page 51)
- crayons or markers
- scissors
- green construction paper
- glue

Hand-clapping games give children an excellent opportunity to develop motor skills, explore rhythm, and cross the midline as they alternately clap with their right and left hands.

Give Your Partner a Hand

SKILLS

Follow directions
Keep a steady beat
Listen
Understand rhythm

Tell children Mary probably played hand-clapping games when she (and her lamb) went to school. Invite children to find a partner. Show children how to sit cross-legged on the floor facing each other so their knees touch. Tell children to clap both hands together. Show children how to use their right hand to clap their partner's right hand. Have children clap their own hands together and then clap their partner's left hand with their own left hand. Play "Mary Had a Little Lamb" as children keep the beat with their hand-clapping pattern.

MATERIALS

- "Mary Had a Little Lamb" (CD 1, Track 15)

Farm Animals

The Little Turtle

There was a little turtle.
He lived in a box.
He swam in a puddle.
He climbed on the rocks.

He snapped at a mosquito.
He snapped at a flea.
He snapped at a minnow.
And he snapped at me!

He caught the mosquito.
He caught the flea.
He caught the minnow.
But he didn't catch me!

Turtle in the Box

Cut a large piece of white construction paper in half widthwise to make a rectangle. Fold a large piece of brown construction paper in half widthwise, and glue the white rectangle inside it. Cut the top piece of construction paper into four equal strips to make a flipbook. Make one flipbook for each child. Play "The Little Turtle," and ask children to recall the animals the turtle snapped at in order. Give each child a Little Turtle in a Box reproducible to color and cut apart. Ask children to write their name on the space in the first box and glue it to the cover of their book. Tell children to open the first construction paper flap of their book to reveal the white paper. Ask children to recall what the turtle snapped at first in the song and glue the paper square with that animal to the white paper. Ask children to open the second flap of their book and glue the paper square that shows what the turtle snapped at next. Continue with the third and fourth sections. Invite children to read their flipbooks to each other.

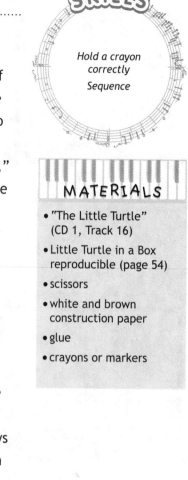

SKILLS

Hold a crayon correctly
Sequence

MATERIALS

- "The Little Turtle" (CD 1, Track 16)
- Little Turtle in a Box reproducible (page 54)
- scissors
- white and brown construction paper
- glue
- crayons or markers

Little Turtle Maze

Give each child a Little Turtle Maze reproducible. Invite children to connect the turtles to the animals at the end of the mazes. After children complete the activity, play "The Little Turtle," and ask children to point to the corresponding pictures on their paper as they sing each part of the song.

SKILLS

Hold a pencil correctly
Sequence
Understand left-to-right orientation
Trace

MATERIALS

- "The Little Turtle" (CD 1, Track 16)
- Little Turtle Maze reproducible (page 55)

Little Turtle in a Box

The Little Turtle

by _____

He snapped at a mosquito.

He snapped at a flea.

He snapped at a minnow.

And he snapped at me!

Little Miss Muffet

Little Miss Muffet
Sat on a tuffet
Eating her curds and whey.
Along came a spider
And sat down beside her
And frightened Miss Muffet away.

When children use all of their senses, several brain connections are stimulated. In this activity, children use four of their senses to learn new vocabulary and develop oral language skills.

A Meal with Miss Muffet

Play "Little Miss Muffet." Show children three cartons of cottage cheese, and explain that each one contains *curds* of a different size. Encourage children to view the contents of each container to determine what curds are. Ask children to name what else Little Miss Muffet was eating in the song. Prompt children to say *whey*, and explain that whey is the watery substance that is left over from making cheese. Spoon a sample of each curd-size cottage cheese on separate crackers for each child. Ask children to sample the cracker with the smallest curds first. Encourage them to touch and smell the cheese before they eat it. Have children describe how the cheese looks, feels, smells, and tastes before they eat the other two crackers.

Learn new vocabulary words

Listen

Understand size relationships

MATERIALS

- "Little Miss Muffet" (CD 1, Track 17)
- cottage cheese (small, medium, and large curd)
- spoon
- crackers

This activity exercises the brain and nervous system and improves tracking skills.

Spider Tracking

Tie a plastic spider or button to the end of a piece of string. Make one for every two children. Invite children to work with a partner. Give one child in each pair a string, and ask him or her to swing it slowly from left to right, right to left, up and down, and back and forth several inches from the face of his or her partner. Encourage the other child to use only his or her eyes to track the "spider" as it swings from its "web."

Concentrate

Follow directions

Track objects

MATERIALS

- plastic spiders or buttons
- 12" (30.5 cm) pieces of string

Hickory Dickory Dock

Hickory, dickory, dock,
The mouse went up the clock.
The clock struck one,
Down he did run.
Hickory, dickory, dock.

Fly—two—away he flew
Frog—three—the frog did flee
Worm—four—he fell to the floor
Bee—five—he flew to the hive
Snake—six—he hid in some sticks
Moth—seven—he flew to the heavens
Cricket—eight—he hid in a crate
Spider—nine—he swung down his line
Mole—ten—he ran to his den
Ant—eleven—he hid behind seven
Elephant—twelve—he let out a yell
And that was the end of the clock.

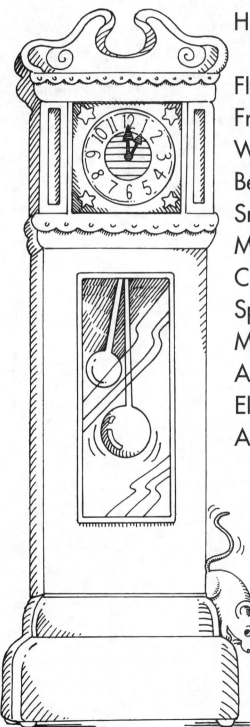

Hickory Dickory Dock Clock

Make twelve copies of the Clock reproducible. Cut out each clock face, and glue each one to a different-colored sheet of construction paper. Cut out all the clock hands, and glue one pair of hands to a clock so that it points to number 1. Continue so that each clock hand points to a different number. Give each child or pair of children a different clock. Play "Hickory Dickory Dock," and encourage children to listen carefully for the number that is indicated on their clock. Tell children to remember the animal that was named with their number. After children listen to the song, have them draw their animal on their clock. Invite children to help you arrange the clocks in numerical order on the floor or on a ledge. Play "Hickory Dickory Dock" again, and invite children to point to the correct clock as it is named in the song.

Count
Recognize numbers from 1-10
Sequence

MATERIALS

- "Hickory Dickory Dock" (CD 1, Track 18)
- Clock reproducible (page 60)
- scissors
- glue
- construction paper (assorted colors)
- crayons or markers

It's About Time

Draw a line down the center of a piece of chart paper. Draw a sun above the left column and a moon above the right column. Make an enlarged copy of the Morning and Night Cards, and cut them apart. Give each card to a child. Invite children who have a card to stand beside the chart one at a time. Ask children to describe the picture on their card and decide whether we do that activity in the morning or at night. Have children tape their card in the correct column. Give each child a set of Morning and Night Cards to color and cut apart. Give each child a construction paper strip, and tell children to write their name at the top. Invite children to glue the pictures in sequential order on their strip of paper.

Make comparisons
Understand opposite word pairs
Print name
Sequence

MATERIALS

- Morning and Night Cards (page 61)
- chart paper
- scissors
- tape and glue
- crayons or markers
- construction paper strips

Clock

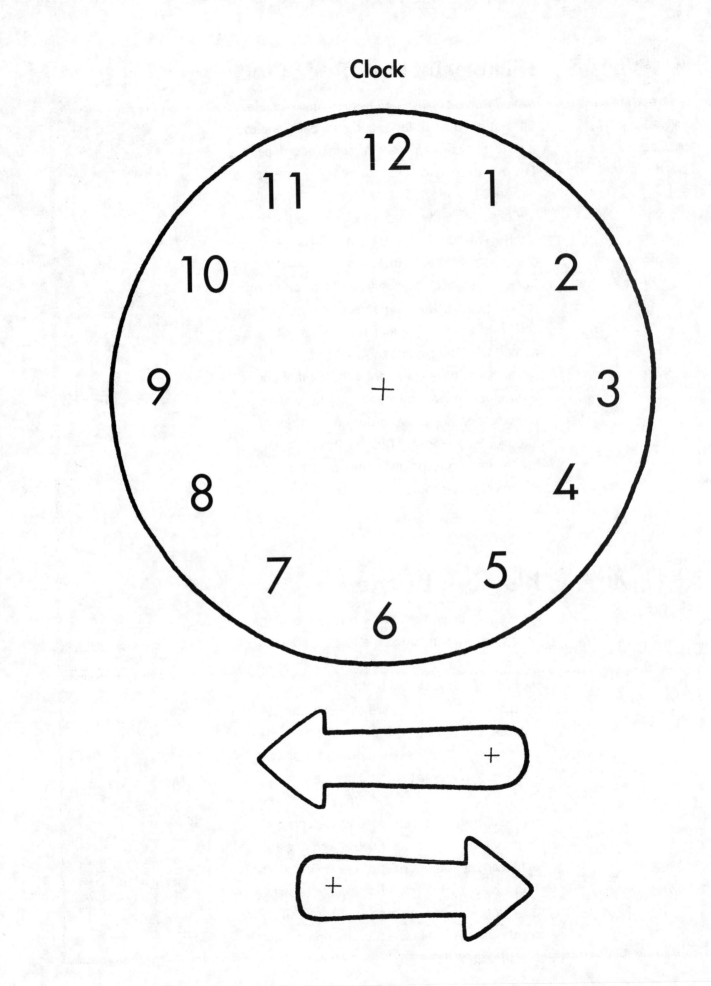

Morning and Night Cards

Six Little Ducks

Six little ducks that I once knew—
Fat ones, skinny ones, fair ones, too.

Chorus:
But the one little duck with a feather on his back.
He led the others with his quack, quack, quack!
Quack, quack, quack! Quack, quack, quack!
He led the others with his quack, quack, quack!

Down to the river they would go.
Wibble, wobble, wibble, wobble, to and fro.

(Chorus)

Home from the river they would come.
Wibble, wobble, wibble, wobble, ho-hum-hum.

(Chorus)

Wibble–Wobble Words

Identify beginning sounds

Isolate beginning sounds

Sing

MATERIALS

- "Six Little Ducks" (CD 1, Track 19; CD 2, Track 18)

Play "Six Little Ducks," and ask children to demonstrate what "wibble" and "wobble" might look like. Encourage children to name and demonstrate the movement of other animals, such as "hippity-hop," "clippity-clop," "wiggle-waggle," and "slip and slide." Combine children's or animal's names with the names of each movement to emphasize alliterative language. For example, you could say *Hannah goes hippity-hop over the hill* or *A walrus wiggle-waggles into the water*. Play the instrumental track of "Six Little Ducks," and encourage children to perform their movements as you use alliteration to describe what they are doing.

Mother and Father Match

Identify beginning sounds

Isolate beginning sounds

Make comparisons

Sort

MATERIALS

- Mother and Father Match reproducible (page 64)
- crayons or markers
- scissors
- file folder
- stapler

Copy, color, and cut apart the Mother and Father Match reproducible. Laminate the cutouts for durability. Write *Make a Match* on the front cover of a file folder. Open the folder, and staple the mother duck to the top left side. Staple the father duck to the top right side. Show children the file folder. Point to the mother duck, and ask *What sound does **mother** begin with?* Invite children to name other words that begin with /m/. Point to the father duck, and ask *What sound does **father** begin with?* Invite children to name other words that begin with /f/. Show children the picture cards. Explain that they should place a card near the mother if it has a picture of a word that begins with /m/ and near the father if it has a picture of a word that begins with /f/. Place the folder and picture cards at a learning center, and invite children to sort the cards by beginning sound.

Mother and Father Match

Pop! Goes the Weasel

All around the cobbler's bench
The monkey chased the weasel.
The monkey thought 'twas all in fun.
Pop! Goes the weasel.

Chorus:
A penny for a spool of thread.
A nickel for a needle;
That's the way the money goes.
Pop! Goes the weasel.

The weasel's pants—too small and too tight—
One button had the weasel.
The monkey pulled with all of his might.
Pop! Goes the weasel.

(Chorus)

His pants fell down to the monkey's delight.

He finally caught the weasel.
They laughed so hard they fell on the floor.
Pop! Goes the weasel.

(Chorus)

He found suspenders to hold up his pants.
No need for thread and needle.
The monkey snapped them on weasel's back.
Pop! Goes the weasel.

The weasel's finally had enough
So now he chases the monkey.
This is how the story ends.
Pop! Goes the monkey.
This is how the story ends.
Pop! Goes the monkey.

Children will develop motor skills and strengthen their left-brain, right-brain connection as they alternate the direction in which they walk and wave their hands. Their concentration will improve as they listen to the changes in the music and respond accordingly.

Pop! Go the Children

Give each child a streamer or scarf. Arrange children in a circle. Play "Pop! Goes the Weasel," and invite children to walk in a circle to the right as they move their streamer or scarf overhead from side to side with their right hand. Tell children to slowly bend to the ground when they hear the words *The monkey thought 'twas all in fun*. Have children jump when they hear *Pop! Goes the weasel*. Ask children to walk in a circle to the left and wave their streamer or scarf with their left hand for the next verse. Remind children to bend down and "pop up" when directed in the song. Continue reversing directions and alternating hands for the duration of the song.

MATERIALS

- "Pop! Goes the Weasel" (CD 1, Tracks 20 and 21)
- streamers or scarves

Children will practice number and coin identification as well as develop memory skills.

Monkey Money Exchange

Play "Pop! Goes the Weasel." Explain to children that a cobbler is someone who makes and sells shoes. Ask children to name some of the objects a cobbler might use in his or her workshop. Give each child a Monkey Money Exchange reproducible. Review with children the value of

a penny, nickel, and dime. Have children identify what each item is and how much it costs. Encourage children to color the coins that could be used to purchase each item.

MATERIALS

- "Pop! Goes the Weasel" (CD 1, Tracks 20 and 21)
- Monkey Money Exchange reproducible (page 67)
- crayons or markers

Name _____

Monkey Money Exchange

Color the coins you could use to buy each item.

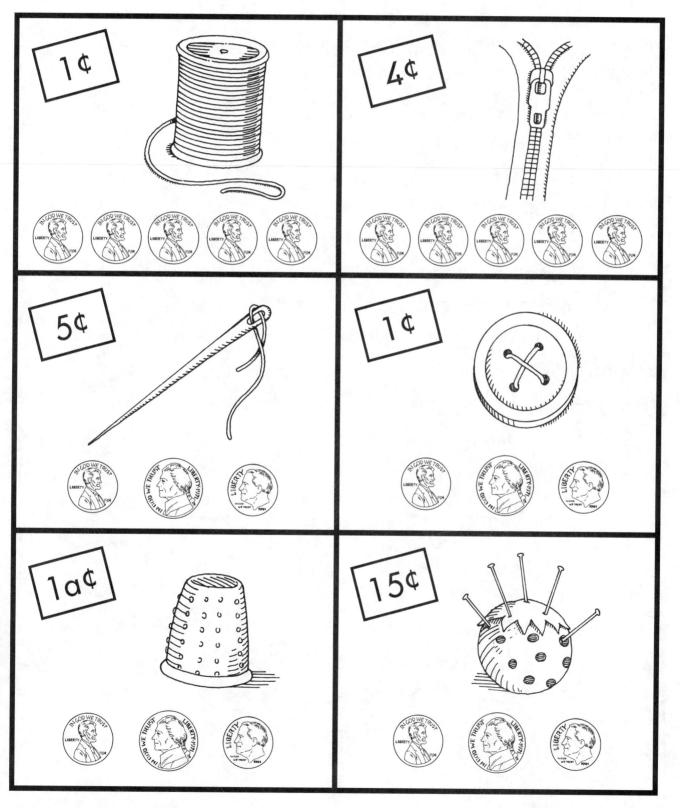

Sing a song of sixpence—a pocket full of rye.
Four and twenty blackbirds baked in a pie.
When the pie was opened the birds began to sing.
Was that not a dainty dish to set before the king?

The king was in his counting house
Counting out his money.
The queen was in the parlor
Eating bread and honey.
The maid was in the garden
Hanging out the clothes
When along came a blackbird
And snipped off her nose!

Sets of Six

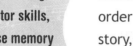

Explain to children that a sixpence is worth six pennies. Play "Sing a Song of Sixpence," and encourage children to listen carefully to the order of events. Invite children to retell the story, and draw a symbol to represent each main part (e.g., coin, birds, pie) in order on chart paper. Ask children to make a movement (e.g., drop coins into hand, flap arms like a bird, knead dough for a pie) for each symbol. Play the song again, and lead children in performing six sets of each movement to the music.

Follow directions
Learn new vocabulary words
Listen
Sequence

MATERIALS

- "Sing a Song of Sixpence" (CD 1, Track 22)
- chart paper

Pie Graph

Ask children to name different kinds of pie they have eaten. Draw several columns on a piece of butcher paper. Draw the fruit or vegetable that is used in children's favorite pies (e.g., pumpkin, pecan, blueberry, cherry, apple, banana, lemon) at the bottom of each column. Give each child an index card, and have children write their name on it. Invite them to place their card in the column that shows their favorite type of pie. Ask them to help you count the number of people who like each kind of pie. Ask children which kind of pie children liked the most and least. Spoon blueberry jam and strawberry jam and mashed bananas on wafer cookies, and give a few to each child. Play "Sing a Song of Sixpence," and invite children to eat their "pies" as they listen to the music.

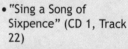

Analyze data
Count
Learn new vocabulary words
Make comparisons

MATERIALS

- "Sing a Song of Sixpence" (CD 1, Track 22)
- butcher paper
- index cards
- blueberry and strawberry jam
- bananas
- wafer cookies

Little boy blue
Come blow your horn.
The sheep's in the meadow.
The cow's in the corn.

But where is the boy
Who looks after the sheep?
He's under the haystack
Fast asleep.

Will you wake him?
No, not I.
For if I do
He's sure to cry.

Cow Count

Copy and cut apart the Cows and Sheep reproducible. Play "Little Boy Blue," and ask children where the cows were in the song. Give each child a paper towel tube and a construction paper strip. Tell children to glue their strip around their tube to make a "horn." Invite children to sit in a circle, and place a piece of yellow construction paper in the middle of the circle. Place the cow and sheep cutouts on the yellow paper. Invite a child to stand, and say *Little boy (or girl) blue, come blow your horn. Can you tell me how many cows there are in the corn?* Tell the child to "blow" his or her horn the same number of times as there are "cows in the corn." Invite a different child to stand, change the number of cows, and repeat the activity.

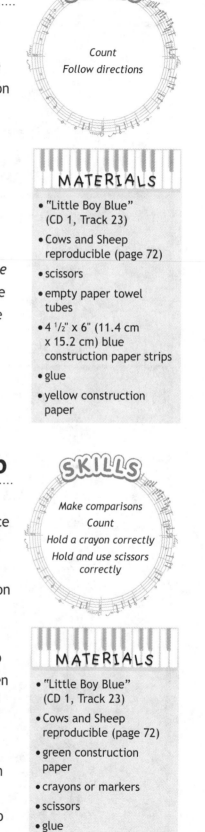

SKILLS

Count
Follow directions

MATERIALS

- "Little Boy Blue" (CD 1, Track 23)
- Cows and Sheep reproducible (page 72)
- scissors
- empty paper towel tubes
- 4 1/2" x 6" (11.4 cm x 15.2 cm) blue construction paper strips
- glue
- yellow construction paper

Counting Cows and Sheep

Play "Little Boy Blue," and ask children where the cows and sheep went. Give each child a piece of green construction paper. Write on the board ____ *sheep in the meadow.* Have children copy the text along the bottom of their paper. Write on the board ____ *cows in the corn.* Have children copy the text along the bottom of the back of their paper. Give each child two Cows and Sheep reproducibles to color and cut apart. Tell children to glue several sheep on the front of their paper and several cows on the back of their paper. Ask them to count the sheep and write the number on the blank line below the sheep. Have children count the cows and write the number on the blank line below the cows. Encourage children to read their sentences to you. Ask them to tell you which side of their paper has more animals.

SKILLS

Make comparisons
Count
Hold a crayon correctly
Hold and use scissors correctly

MATERIALS

- "Little Boy Blue" (CD 1, Track 23)
- Cows and Sheep reproducible (page 72)
- green construction paper
- crayons or markers
- scissors
- glue

Cows and Sheep

Old MacDonald Had a Farm

Old MacDonald had a farm.
E-I-E-I-O!
And on his farm he had some chicks.
E-I-E-I-O!
With a chick, chick here,
And a chick, chick there.
Here a chick, there a chick,
Everywhere a chick, chick.
Old MacDonald had a farm.
E-I-E-I-O!

Cows—moo, moo
Pigs—oink, oink
Sheep—baa, baa
Ducks—quack, quack

Old MacDonald's Bottle Band

Invite children to arrange bottles in order by ascending size. Use a permanent marker to label each bottle of the same size with the same number. Give each child an empty bottle. Show children how to blow across the opening of their bottle to create a sound. Tell children to take periodic rests from blowing their "wind instrument" so they can catch their breath. Prompt them to determine that the larger bottles make lower sounds. Invite children with the same number to stand together. Invite each group to make a musical pattern for the other groups to follow. Play "Old MacDonald Had a Farm," and encourage children to play along on their bottle.

SKILLS

Make patterns

Recognize numbers from 1-10

Understand rhythm

Understand size relationships

MATERIALS

- "Old MacDonald Had a Farm" (CD 1, Track 24)
- clean, empty, plastic water or soda bottles of various sizes
- permanent marker

Phonemic Fun on the Farm

Copy, color, and cut apart the Farm Animals reproducible. Glue a piece of felt to the back of each animal. Scatter the animals on the floor beneath a felt board. Invite children to sit in view of the board. Sing the first verse of "Old MacDonald Had a Farm," but in the last line omit the name of an animal. Instead, say the sounds of the animal's name (e.g., /c/ /a/ /t/). Invite a child to identify the animal and place it on the felt board. Encourage children to continue singing the song with the sound the animal makes. Repeat the process with a new animal and a different child.

SKILLS

Isolate beginning sounds

Listen

MATERIALS

- Farm Animals reproducible (page 51)
- crayons
- scissors
- glue
- felt
- felt board

Hey Diddle Diddle

Hey diddle diddle
The cat and the fiddle.
The cow jumped over the moon.
The little dog laughed to see such sport.
And the dish ran away with the spoon.

Fiddling with Nouns and Verbs

Play "Hey Diddle Diddle," and ask children to describe the actions of the animals and objects in the song. Ask children if a cat could really play a fiddle, a cow could jump over the moon, a dog could laugh, and a dish could run away with a spoon. Have children describe how these animals really behave and how we use these objects. Give each child a Hey Diddle Diddle reproducible to color. Ask children to cut apart the cards at the bottom of their paper. Ask them to point to the picture of the thumb pointing down. Tell children to glue the cards that show something that cannot really happen below this picture. Ask them to point to the picture of the thumb pointing up. Tell children to glue the cards that show something that really can happen below this picture. When children have completed their work, invite them to explain why they put their cards where they did.

SKILLS

Learn new vocabulary words
Make comparisons
Sort

MATERIALS

- "Hey Diddle Diddle" (CD 1, Track 25)
- Hey Diddle Diddle reproducible (page 77)
- crayons or markers
- scissors
- glue

Rubber-Band Band

Secure one end of a large rubber band around the toe of your shoe to make a "fiddle." Gradually stretch and loosen the rubber band as you tap it with a pencil. Invite individual children to use the pencil to tap the rubber band as you change the tension. Encourage children to describe the various pitches. Assign different children an animal from the song to pantomime. Play "Hey Diddle Diddle," and encourage children to imitate the actions of their animal as they sing the song.

SKILLS

Keep a steady beat
Follow directions

MATERIALS

- "Hey Diddle, Diddle" (CD 1, Track 25)
- rubber band
- pencil

Hey Diddle Diddle

The cat came piping out of the barn
With a set of bagpipes under her arm.
She could sing nothing but "Fiddle-de-dee.
The mouse will marry the bumblebee."
Cat plays bagpipes.
Bee dances with mouse.
We'll have the wedding at our good house.

The cat came piping out of the barn
As the cow and the sow danced arm in arm.
The ducks in their waistcoats served biscuits and tea
For the mouse had married the bumblebee.
They'll live in a hole
In the old chestnut tree.
Fiddle-de-dee, fiddle-de-dee.

Mother Goose Brain Boost © 2006 Creative Teaching Press

This activity stimulates coordination on both sides, helping children cross the midline between the left and right hemispheres of their brains and between the top and the bottom of their bodies.

These Cats Can Catch

Give each child a beanbag, a small ball, or a sheet of paper that has been rolled up into a ball. Show children how to toss it from hand to hand. Tell children to pretend they are cats scratching something, and have them catch the object with their palm facing down. Play "The Cat Came Piping out of the Barn" as they practice throwing and catching in this way.

Throw and catch a ball

MATERIALS

- "The Cat Came Piping out of the Barn" (CD 1, Track 26)
- beanbags, small balls, or rolled-up sheets of paper

Young children are primarily kinesthetic learners. In this activity, they will develop fine motor skills as they learn a new vocabulary word.

The Cat Came Piping

Give each child a Cat's Pipes reproducible. Tell children to color the sections that contain uppercase letters to reveal the instrument the cat plays in "The Cat Came Piping out of the Barn." After children color their picture, play the song to give children an "auditory" picture of bagpipes to complement the visual one they created on their paper.

Hold a crayon correctly
Identify letters

MATERIALS

- "The Cat Came Piping out of the Barn" (CD 1, Track 26)
- Cat's Pipes reproducible (page 80)
- crayons or markers

Cat's Pipes

Color the sections that contain uppercase letters to reveal the instrument the cat played.

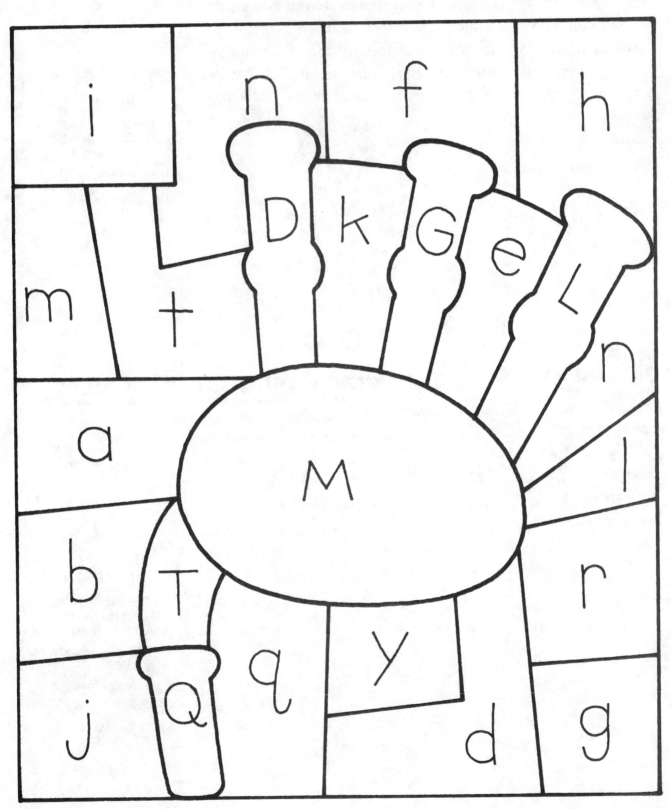